The Stinky Wonky Donkey

Words by **Craig Smith**

Illustrations by **Katz Cowley**

■ SCHOLASTIC

There was a young donkey,
so cute and small,
who loved every creature,
from tiny to tall.

"I love every animal,
of that there's no doubt.
I love them so much,"
Dinky Donkey called out.

The Stinky Wonky Donkey

For my beautiful girl, Maia.
And for all the dads who
try to bring more fun
into their family's lives.
– Craig Smith

To marvellous Mary of the Unicorns and Lucy Platypus,
for helping to bring this book-baby into being ...
and to every child who reads this: may you always
know the love and guidance of the Creator.
– Katz Cowley

Published in the UK by Scholastic, 2023
1 London Bridge, London, SE1 9BG
Scholastic Ireland, 89E Lagan Road, Dublin Industrial Estate, Glasnevin, Dublin, D11 HP5F

SCHOLASTIC and associated logos are trademarks and/or
registered trademarks of Scholastic Inc.

First published in New Zealand by Scholastic New Zealand, 2023

Text © Craig Smith, 2023
Illustrations © Katz Cowley, 2023

The right of Craig Smith and Katz Cowley to be identified
as the author and illustrator of this work has been asserted
by them under the Copyright, Designs and Patents Act 1988.

ISBN 978 0702 32591 5

A CIP catalogue record for this book is available from the British Library.

Printed in Italy
Paper made from wood grown in sustainable forests and other controlled sources.

1 3 5 7 9 10 8 6 4 2

www.scholastic.co.uk

"Really?" said Wonky.
"Which do you love best?
Which animals do you love
more than the rest?"

"I don't really know,"
wee Dinky confessed.
"I've never thought which I love
MORE than the rest."

She hee'd and she hawed,
and pondered a while,
she shook her wee mane ...
then, with a big smile,
"Reindeer," she said,
"and donkeys that bray,
stampeding warthogs –
out of their way!"

"I love hippopotamus,
zebras and goats.
I love beautiful horses
with smooth, glossy coats.
With all of my heart,
I love lambs too,
camels and antelopes,
and cows that go MOO!"

And as Wonky listened,
his face was deadpan,
but he was devising
an outrageous plan!

"Those animals that you love so much,
the reindeer, horses, camels and such,
they have one thing in common,
and it's not their moves ...
Can you guess what it is?
They all have HOOVES!"

"You love hoofed animals
with all your heart,
that makes you *hoof-hearted*,"
he said, feeling smart.

"Hoof-hearted, hoof-hearted!
Without a doubt!
I *am* hoof-hearted,"
Dinky called out.

Her daddy then brayed aloud happily.
"Is your Granny hoof-hearted?"
he asked with glee.

Off Dinky trotted,
and was back in a tick.
"Granny says she's hoof-hearted,
then had a giggling fit!"

Laughing some more,
Wonky then said,
"Go and ask Mummy.
She's out in the shed!"

Away Dinky ran, then back she darted.
"Yes, Daddy," she said.
"Mummy's also hoof-hearted!"

"I'm glad she's admitted it,"
he said with a guffaw.
Dinky's dad was now rolling
around on the floor!

Then he slowly got up,
saying, "Oh no ... no more!"
and he headed outside,
through the stable door.

Catching him quickly,
before he departed,
Dinky asked, "Daddy ...
are you hoof-hearted?"

"Well, Dinky," said Wonky,
"to tell you the truth
and to answer your question ...

here ... pull my hoof!"

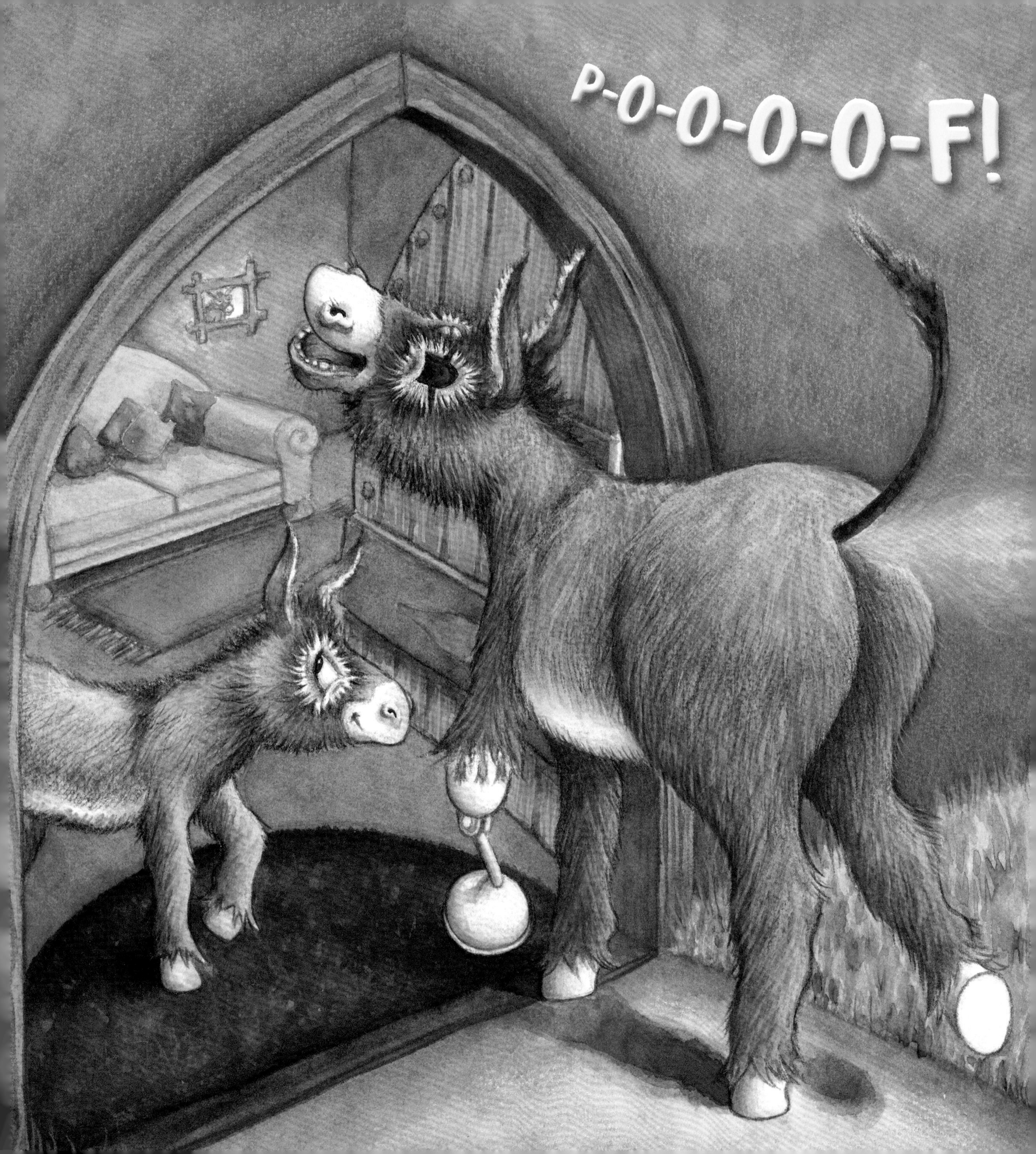
P-O-O-O-O-F!